Contents

OSWALD
the Silly Goose

K. R. Whittington

Illustrated by Tony Escott

Bradbury Press

Scarsdale, New York

First published 1974
© Text K. R. Whittington 1974
© Illustrations Wm. Collins Sons & Co. Ltd. 1974

Library of Congress Catalog Card Number: 73-89222

Printed in Great Britain by William Collins Sons & Co. Ltd.,
London and Glasgow
First American edition published by Bradbury Press, Inc., 1974

ISBN: 0-87888-067-4   First printing

The text of this book is set in 14 pt. Baskerville
The illustrations are pencil drawings reproduced by litho

Oswald and the Worm Seeds

One day Oswald, the silly goose, went to his worm patch to dig up some worms for breakfast. Because the weather had been very hot and dry, all the worms were deep underground and Oswald could not find any. "Ah," he thought, "this season's crop of worms is finished; I shall have to plant some more seeds." "Don't be stupid!" said Mrs. Oswald, his wife. "Worms don't grow from seeds," and she hit him on the head with her rolling pin just to make

5

sure he remembered that. But Oswald went around to Mouse's Flower and Seed Shop and asked Shopkeeper Mouse for two pennyworth of worm seeds. "Don't be stupid!" said Shopkeeper Mouse. "Everyone knows that worms don't grow from seeds." But Oswald was still sure that worms did grow from seeds, so he decided to make some for himself, out of mud. He mixed a large quantity of earth from the garden with water in Mrs. Oswald's best mixing bowl, and added two eggs for good measure. "Things are more likely to hatch out, with eggs," he thought vaguely. Then he spread the mixture on the kitchen

table and rolled it into little balls. Most of the mud went over the kitchen floor, and Oswald trod in it and made muddy footmarks all over Mrs. Oswald's best carpet. But he did succeed in making about twenty worm seeds, which he carefully carried outside and planted in his worm patch.

When Mrs. Oswald returned home she asked what he had been doing. "Planting worm seeds," said Oswald. "Don't be stupid!" said Mrs. Oswald. "Worms don't grow from seeds!" And she hit him on the head with her rolling pin to make sure he remembered that.

Every day Oswald carefully watered his worm seeds. After a week he decided it was time to harvest the worms. He fetched his spade, and in no time at all collected a bucketful. Of course, the worms had really come to the top because of all the water Oswald had poured on the ground every day, but Oswald thought they had grown from his seeds.

He showed the bucketful of worms to Mrs. Oswald. "Worms don't grow from seeds!" she cried, and hit him on the head with her rolling pin to make sure he remembered that.

So Oswald ate all the worms himself.

Oswald at the Spider Show

One day, while he was out for a walk, Oswald saw
a notice saying:

GRAND SPIDER SHOW

BIG PRIZES

ENTRY FORMS FROM ORGANIZER MOUSE

Now Oswald thought he knew all about spiders, and he determined to enter and win first prize. He got an entry form from Mouse, then hurried home and looked in his spider cupboard. He chose the biggest, hairiest spider and put it in a box by itself.

For the next week Oswald carefully groomed his spider every day. He brushed it and combed it,

and fed it with a specially large fly each morning. At the end of the week the spider was ENORMOUS, and GLEAMED from head to foot.

But the following day when Oswald went to groom his spider, it had disappeared. He looked everywhere for it: under the sofa, behind the sink,

down the drain. Finally he asked Mrs. Oswald:
"Have you seen my spider?" "Yes," she said.
"I baked it in a pie this morning." "But that was
my prize spider for the Show!" cried Oswald. "You
can't expect me to know that," said Mrs. Oswald,

and she not only hit Oswald on the head with her rolling pin to teach him not to be stupid, she also ate the pie all by herself.

Next day Oswald selected the second-best spider from his cupboard and put it in the box. He groomed it and fed it with *two* flies every day, and carefully hid it where Mrs. Oswald could not find it. By the fourth day this spider was even bigger than the first one, and its coat shone even more brightly.

On the fifth day Oswald fed his spider as usual, but forgot to close the box. The next time he went to feed it, it had GONE ! !

There were now only three days left before the Spider Show. Oswald selected one more spider, and

this time he not only brushed it and combed it, he shampooed it as well, and fed it *three* fat flies every day. By the day of the Show it was even bigger than the first two spiders, and its coat was DAZZLING.

Oswald packed it in his lunch-bag and set off for the showground, where the exhibits were already arranged in the big tent. There were prizes for the best arrangement of five spiders, for the spider with the hairiest legs, and for the champion fly-catcher of the season. But best of all, there was to be the grand prize for the Outright Winner of the Show. Oswald went to find Mouse. "Here's my entry," he said. "Bound to win." "Where's your entry form?" asked Mouse. "You can't enter unless you've filled in your form."

Oswald went cold all over: he had left his entry form at home! He rushed out of the tent, and saw Orange Bird standing outside. "Hold this for me!" shouted Oswald, dropping his spider at Orange Bird's feet, and he dashed home.

But when Oswald returned with his entry form he was too late. The judging had started, and no one was allowed in the tent. "Where's my spider, anyway?" he asked Orange Bird. "Well," said Orange Bird, "I got hungry . . ."

When the judging was over, Oswald wandered in miserably to see who had won. The Outright

Winner of the Show, with a big FIRST PRIZE label, was a large hairy spider with a shining, beautifully groomed coat. As Oswald looked at the Outright Winner, a great suspicion entered his head. He peered more closely. It was *his* spider. "It's my second spider, the one that escaped," thought Oswald. "Someone must have found it and put it in for the Show!" Just then Mouse came in for the prize-giving. After giving out the less important prizes, he said: "Now, for the proud owner of the Outright Winner of this Show." "That's my spider!" shouted Oswald, but nobody took any notice.

"I would like to present this grand prize," said Mouse, to MRS. OSWALD!"

"But that's *my* spider!" shouted Oswald.

"Well," snapped Mrs. Oswald, as she unwrapped her prize, a brand new rolling pin, "ARE YOU GOING TO ARGUE ABOUT IT?"

"In future," thought Oswald unhappily, "I shall stick to *eating* spiders, not putting them in Shows."

Oswald Goes Swimming

One day Oswald decided to go swimming. He made himself some worm and caterpillar sandwiches and wrapped them in a towel with his bathing trunks in case he got hungry. He also put a few spiders in his pocket, in case he got even hungrier. Then he went to catch the bus to the swimming pool.

18

There were a lot of people at the bus stop. Oswald stood at the end of the line and waited patiently. When the bus came all the people in front

of Oswald got on, but just as Oswald was about to step forward the conductor shouted, "Full up!" and off went the bus.

Oswald waited and waited, and more people came and formed a line behind him. When at last another bus came along, he leaped forward, tripped over the step, and fell flat on his face. All his sandwiches fell out of his towel into the gutter. A fat lady trod on one and, as Oswald grovelled about in the gutter, trying to pick them up, all the people behind him got on the bus. At last Oswald

had collected all his sandwiches and put them back in his towel. "Full up!" shouted the conductor, and rang the bell. Off went the bus, leaving Oswald sitting in the gutter.

When the next bus came Oswald managed to

get on and sat down, putting his sandwiches on the seat beside him. A portly gentleman came along and sat on them.

Then Conductor Mouse came along to collect the fares. "Swimming pool, please," said Oswald.

"Five pennies," said Mouse. "Well, um, er," replied Oswald. "I seem to have left my money at home." "Then you'll have to get off," said Mouse. "Oh no I won't," said Oswald, who was determined to get to the swimming pool this time. "Look, Goose," said

Conductor Mouse. "If you don't get off I'll throw you off." "Oh no you won't," said Oswald, who didn't think Mouse would. So Mouse did.

It wasn't until Oswald had picked himself up and saw the bus disappearing into the distance that he realized his swimming things were still on board.

"Give me back my swimming things!" shouted Oswald, rushing after the bus. Every time the bus stopped Oswald gained a little, but it always drew away again before he could catch up. Finally the bus was held up in a traffic jam and Oswald, puffing and blowing, drew level with it. Conductor Mouse eyed him coldly. "You're not getting on this bus again, Goose," he said. "Give – puff – me – puff – my – puff – swimming things!" gasped Oswald. "You're welcome to them," said Mouse and threw the towel, with the swimming trunks and sandwiches still wrapped up inside, into the road. Before Oswald could pick it up, a truck ran over it.

Mrs. Mouse was behind the ticket counter at the swimming pool. "I'm sorry," she said, "we're closed." "Look," said Oswald. "I've come all this way. I've missed two buses. I've been thrown off another one. I've had my sandwiches run over by a truck. AND I'M GOING SWIMMING. And," he added rudely, "I've had enough trouble today with your stupid husband!" He pushed past Mrs. Mouse and went into the changing room.

Oswald had just changed into his bathing costume (liberally smeared with breadcrumbs and

squashed caterpillars) when two bath attendants rushed in. "Come back, Goose!" they shouted. "You can't go in there!" But Oswald didn't wait. He dashed out of the changing room, up the ladder to the top diving board, and launched himself into space. It wasn't until he was half-way down that he realized why the swimming pool was closed. It had been emptied for cleaning.

Oswald landed with a dull thud and bent his beak badly. "Oh well," he thought, as the two attendants carried him off on a stretcher, "I never did like getting wet, anyway!"

Oswald and the Glue

One day Oswald woke up feeling very hungry, and decided to make some porridge for his breakfast. He rushed downstairs to the kitchen, took a packet of porridge out of the cupboard and emptied it into some water in a saucepan. Now, it was really glue powder in the packet and not porridge, but Oswald didn't know this because he hadn't bothered to read the label.

26

When the saucepan came to the boil, the glue spilled all over the hot stove and there was a horrible burning smell. Oswald tried to wipe the hot glue off the stove with his wing. There was another horrible burning smell as all his wing feathers caught fire.

Oswald rushed to the refridgerator and put his wing inside to cool it. Now, when he had finished his supper the night before, he had piled all the dirty plates and dishes in the refridgerator, so that Mrs. Oswald should not see them and order him to wash them up. The glue on his feathers stuck to them, and when he pulled his wing out again, all the plates and dishes fell on the floor and broke.

The saucepan of glue was still boiling over, so Oswald poured it into a big basin. Most of it went over the floor and he trod in it. Then he sat down

at the table and ate the glue in one big sluuurrpp! "Hmm," thought Oswald. "This porridge tastes funny." Suddenly he found he couldn't open his beak. "Ewp! Ewp!" he squawked. He meant to say "Help, Help," but the two halves of his beak were stuck together. Oswald jumped up, and fell flat on his face, because his feet were stuck to the floor. At this moment Mrs. Oswald came in. "Ewp! Ewp!" squawked Oswald again, "Mew bewk ews ewp!" "What are you talking about?" snapped Mrs. Oswald, and she hit Oswald on the head with her rolling pin, just to teach him to speak more clearly.

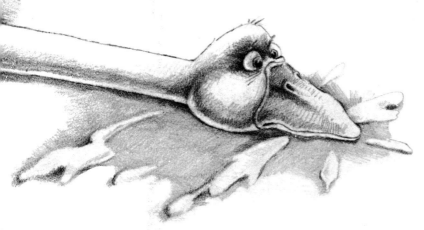

Oswald managed to get his feet free by cutting through the linoleum with the carving knife, but he couldn't get his beak unstuck, so he went around to Rabbit's house. "Ewp mew!" he said. "Mew bewk ews ewp whoop gew." "Shocking cold you have," said Rabbit.

So Oswald had to go to the Doctor's, because nobody heard him properly or understood what he was trying to say. "Goose, Goose," said Doctor Mouse, "What is it you want?" "Mmve gewp ee bewk dewp ewp," said Oswald. "Pardon?" said Doctor Mouse. "I'll test you for a new pair of glasses." Oswald danced up and down in rage. "EWP GEWP!" he screamed. "GEWP EWP MEWP DEWP EW!!!" At last Doctor Mouse understood. "Well, Goose," he said, "Go home and put your beak in hot water. Three times a day after meals," he added, as an afterthought. "Ewk Ewp!" gabbled Oswald, and rushed home.

Mrs. Oswald was in the kitchen boiling a saucepan of water for a spider-bottling session. Oswald snatched the lid off and plunged his beak into the boiling water. A moment later he snatched it out again, quacking loudly: "Oh my beak, oh my

30

beak, oh my poor, poor beak." Oswald's beak was badly scalded, and swollen and sore. He had to stay in bed for several days with a large bandage around it.

"But," thought Oswald, "at least it isn't stuck together any more!"

Oswald and the Submarine

One day Oswald went to the caterpillar and chip shop and bought ten pennyworth of caterpillars wrapped in an old newspaper. When he got home he emptied the caterpillars on the floor and ate them one by one while he looked through the newspaper they had been wrapped in. It contained a picture of a submarine – something Oswald had never seen before. He showed it to Mrs. Oswald. "Look what

I've found," he said. "What is it?" "Education is the thief of time," said Mrs. Oswald, and hit him on the head with her rolling pin, to teach him not to read when he should be washing-up.

Oswald didn't think this was a very helpful reply, so he went around to Rabbit's house with the newspaper. "What's this?" he asked. "It's a boat that goes under the water," said Rabbit. "If it goes under the water," said Oswald, "how do you get on it?" "Well," said Rabbit. "You can make it come up to the top, or go down to the bottom." "That would be very useful," said Oswald, "because of the worms." "Oh?" said Rabbit, blankly. "Yes," said Oswald. "Worms live in mud, and there is mud at the bottom of the river, so there must be lots of worms there, and you could go down in a submarine and collect them."

Oswald thought a lot about the submarine, and decided to make one. Several days later Rabbit found him down by the river with an old wooden

barrel labelled "Best English Salted Spiders". "Will you help me?" asked Oswald, and he explained how it worked. "I have drilled two holes in this barrel. One is to let the water in, and the other is to let it out. So, if I cover one hole up, the boat will go down, and if I cover the other, it will go up." "Really?" asked Rabbit, doubtfully. "How does the

water know which hole is which?" "Easy," said Oswald. "I have labelled them. Now nail me in, please." So Rabbit nailed the lid on the barrel, and threw it, with Oswald inside, into the river.

The first part of Oswald's plan worked very well. He covered up one of the holes, and water rushed into the other hole and nearly filled the barrel, so that Oswald had great difficulty in keeping his head out of the water. As the barrel was made of wood, it didn't sink to the bottom, but bobbed around just below the surface and drifted slowly down the river, rolling over and over.

Oswald, who didn't know what was happening because it was pitch dark inside the barrel, was tumbled head over heels, and began to feel very seasick. "What a long way down," he thought. "The river must be very deep. Surely I'll reach the bottom soon."

After a while, the barrel stuck in some brambles at the side of the river. When it stopped, Oswald thought it had reached the river bed. "Now I can get the worms!" he thought. But this was not as easy as he had expected. First, he couldn't get out of the barrel because the lid was nailed on. Second, the holes were too small for him to reach through.

"Never mind," thought Oswald. "I will go back up and get a stick with a pin on the end. Then I can spear the worms with it through the holes." He covered up the hole marked "Down" and uncovered the hole marked "Up", and waited for the water to drain out. Unfortunately, even more water came in, and soon Oswald could only keep the tip of his beak out of the water by standing on tiptoe. When he opened his beak to shout for help he swallowed large quantities of water which made him cough and splutter. Poor Oswald! All he could do was keep quite still and wait for help to arrive.

It so happened that Mrs. Oswald was walking along the river bank at this time, returning from market with a large basket of juicy worms for tea. She spotted the barrel stuck in the brambles, and read the label on it. "Ah!" she exclaimed. "Best English Salted Spiders! I wonder if it is full?" She pulled the barrel over to the side with her umbrella and, with some difficulty, rolled it on to dry land. "It is certainly very heavy," she thought. "It must be full of spiders." And she pried the lid off.

Out leaped Oswald. He was soaking wet from head to toe, feathers bedraggled and covered in slime from the river and spider fluff from the inside of the barrel. He looked such a sight that Mrs. Oswald didn't recognize him. "Help! Help! a horrible sea-serpent!" she shrieked, dropped the basket of worms and didn't stop running until she reached home.

Oswald sat down and gobbled up all the worms. "Another successful enterprise!" he said.

Oswald the Baby Sitter

One day, when Oswald was even more short of money than usual, he saw a card in the window of Mouse's shop saying "Reliable baby-sitter wanted. Supper provided. Television. Apply Mrs. Rabbit." "Ah," thought Oswald, "I could do that." He especially liked the bit about supper being provided. It didn't occur to him that he knew nothing at all about babies.

"Are you sure you've done this sort of thing before?" asked Mrs. Rabbit doubtfully, when

Oswald applied for the job. "Oh yes," said Oswald. "I'm quite capable." "Well then," said Mrs. Rabbit, "your dinner is in the oven and baby's dinner is in the refridgerator. If he wakes up, change him. I'll be back about ten o'clock."

As soon as Mrs. Rabbit had gone Oswald went into the living room to try the television set. He had

never watched television before and was not sure what to do. He switched on and twiddled all the knobs. A very jumpy pattern of lines appeared. Oswald sat and watched this for some time. "I don't really understand these Modern Art programs," he thought, and tried to switch to another station, but the knob fell off. Oswald banged and kicked the set a few times, but nothing happened, so he pried off the cover with a spade he found in the tool shed, and started poking about inside. There was a loud

bang and thick black smoke started to come out of the front. "This is more interesting," said Oswald, and settled down in the arm-chair to watch.

Soon the baby started crying. "If it wakes up, change it," thought Oswald, so he lifted it out of its

crib and carried it into the garden. Over the fence he could see Mrs. Pig's baby lying in the sun. "I'll change it for that one," he thought. He swopped the baby rabbit for the baby pig, and carried the baby pig upstairs and put it in Baby Rabbit's crib. Baby

Pig started to cry, and Oswald wondered what to do next. "I can't keep *on* changing them," he said to himself. "Perhaps I'll give it a bath." He started running the hot water, and while it was running he decided to have his dinner. "Now let me think," said Oswald. "My dinner is in the refridgerator and the baby's dinner is in the oven."

Oswald took the dinner out of the oven first. It was a steak and kidney pie. Oswald took this upstairs, with a knife and fork, and left it in the baby's crib for Baby Pig to get on with. In the refridgerator he found a bottle of milk and some carrot juice. "Hmm," he thought, "I would have preferred some steak and kidney pie. Still, if I mix these together and add some worms, perhaps it won't

taste too bad." He went into the garden, dug some worms out of Mrs. Rabbit's petunia bed (destroying several petunias in the process), and put them on the stove to boil in a saucepan with the milk and the carrot juice.

Just then Oswald noticed a sound like running water in the living room. It was difficult to see what was happening as the smoke from the television set was so thick, but Oswald could just spy a steady trickle of water coming through the ceiling and collecting in a large pool on the carpet. "Funny," he said. "I wonder where that's coming from?" It didn't occur to him to turn off the bath water.

Instead, he ran into the kitchen, fetched a teacup, and stood it underneath the stream of water. The cup was soon filled up and overflowed, so

Oswald ran and fetched another one. When he had ten full teacups there were no more left in the kitchen, so he started to empty the full ones out on to the carpet, in order to re-use them. Then he hit on the idea of soaking the water up, which he tried to do first with the tablecloth, and then with the sheets off Mrs. Rabbit's bed. As each cloth became water-logged, Oswald would wring it out into the teacups,

then empty the teacups on the floor. It became apparent that the water was rapidly gaining on him, so Oswald looked around desperately for some other means of dealing with it. "I know," he said, "I will vacuum it up!" He plugged in the vacuum cleaner and directed the nozzle at the rapidly growing pool of water. There was a slurping sound, and a very loud BANG, and all the lights went out.

At ten o'clock Mrs. Rabbit came home to a pitch
dark house. She rushed into the smoke-filled living
room and fell flat on her face in a knee-deep pool of
water. Struggling to her feet she lit a candle. In the

48

kitchen there was a horrible smell of burnt milk and worms. In the baby's room a small pink pig sat howling in a dish of steak and kidney pie. In the other bedroom lay Oswald, fast asleep on Mrs. Rabbit's bed.

"WHATEVER'S GOING ON?" shouted Mrs. Rabbit, shaking him.

"Oh, it's you," said Oswald, waking up. "I'll be going now. I'll have my wages now, and can you write me a reference please?"

Oswald Goes Shopping

One day Mrs. Oswald sent her husband into town to do the shopping. "I know you are a silly and scatterbrained goose," she said, "but I have written out this shopping list very clearly, so there is no excuse for you to get it wrong."

Oswald read the shopping list carefully. This took him a long time because he could not read very well. It said:

> 2 Tins Baked Bees
> 1 Jar Pickled Spiders
> Mint Sauce
> 2 Plum Pies
> 1 Pint Caterpillar Sauce
> 500 Beak-ache Pills
> 1 Jar Worm Jam.

Oswald put the list in his pocket and went to catch the bus.

On the bus he met Hedgehog. "Can you tell me the way to the Town Hall, Oswald?" asked Hedgehog. Oswald had no idea where the Town Hall was, but he did not like to appear ignorant. "Of course!" he said. "I will draw you a map!"

Oswald drew a very good map, on the back of the shopping list. It had everything that a good map should have, like rivers, and bridges, and palm trees, and an island with "Treasure" marked on it. "Thank you," said Hedgehog, and got off the bus, taking the map with him.

When Oswald arrived at the grocer's, of course he couldn't find his shopping list. "Funny," he thought. "Never mind, I expect I can remember what was on it. Two tins of baked spiders, please." When Oswald came to pay for the spiders, he found

he had left his money at home. He had only enough to pay for one tin. "Well," he said, "I shall take one tin with me and you can keep the other until I come back."

Then he went to the delicatessen. "I know there was a jar of baked jam," he said to himself,

"Or was it pickled sauce? One jar of caterpillar squashies," he said, at length, making a wild guess. "Where's your money, then," said Mrs. Mouse, who was serving. "I'm sorry," said Oswald. "I haven't any money, but if you let me take the caterpillar squashies with me, I will give you this tin of baked spiders in exchange, until I come back."

Next Oswald went to the butcher's. "Some minced horse and two plump eyes, please," he said, and added, "I will give you this jar of caterpillar squashies in exchange, until I come back with some money."

Next he went to buy the beak-ache pills. "I want a . . . a pint of beak-ache tins," he said. "Or was it a tin of pickled beak-ache jars?" "We only sell beak-ache pills in large bottles," said Miss Mouse, who was serving. "No," said Oswald, confused, "I'm sure it wasn't bottles." "Well," said Miss Mouse, "if you have a beak-ache, I can give you one tablet for

nothing." So Oswald swallowed the tablet, although he didn't have a beak-ache, and went back to the grocer's.

"I want five hundred jars of worm jam," said Oswald, "and I will give you this meat as a deposit."

The jam filled a very large cardboard box. It was much too heavy for Oswald to carry, so he had to push it out into the street. Half-way across the road it got stuck, and Oswald could not shift it. He began to take the jars out, one by one, and to run backwards and forwards, carrying them to the pavement. All this caused a great traffic hold-up, and Police Mouse came along to see what was happening. "'Ere 'ere 'ere, wot's all this?" he

asked. "Let me 'elp you with that there!" He grasped the cardboard box in both arms, and lifted it up. The bottom fell out and all the pots of jam fell into the road, where most of them broke. "Thank you very much," said Oswald politely. "Can you direct me to the Town Hall?" asked Hedgehog, who had suddenly appeared on the scene.

When Oswald got home, Mrs. Oswald asked him where the groceries were. Oswald opened the bag. Inside were three broken jars of worm jam. "You've made a hash of it again!" cried Mrs. Oswald, seizing her rolling pin. "Yes," said Oswald, heading for the door, "but at least I didn't spend very much money!"

A Tail-Piece about Mice

Some people reading these stories may have wondered about all the mice: Fire Mouse, Police Mouse, Bus Conductor Mouse, and so on. They are not the first to have asked where they all came from. At a meeting in the Town Hall, Rabbit stood up and asked why all the important official positions should be filled by mice. Councillor Mouse immediately said this question was Out of Order and instructed Mrs. Oswald to hit Rabbit on the head with a rolling pin, to teach him not to be impertinent. However, there was such an outcry about the matter that a Public Enquiry was set up, and some amazing facts came to light.

In the first place, it turned out that there was *only one mouse*. Mouse changed from one job to another by dashing backwards and forwards and

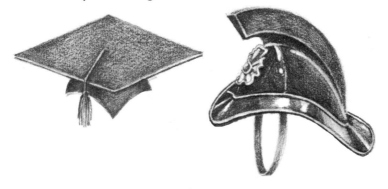

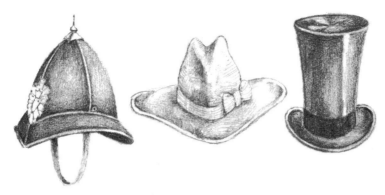

putting on different hats. This explained why it was so difficult to call out the fire brigade when the buses were running, and why a Policemouse could never be found while the mail was being delivered.

However, there were some good things about this arrangement. It did mean that help was always at hand if a bus caught fire, although not as quickly as might be thought, since Bus Conductor Mouse first had to dash home and put on his Firemouse's hat to become Fire Mouse. Then he had to dash back again and put on his Policemouse's hat, to take down everyone's name and address.

Mouse became so fit through dashing backwards and forwards, that he also became Olympic Champion Runner Mouse.

In order to make it easier for him to change

jobs, Mouse built a network of tunnels connecting the Fire Station with the Police Station, the Bus Station, the Post Office and so on. This provided a lot of work for Mouse's Power Shovel and Tunnelling Company. In the end there were so many tunnels underneath the town that part of it caved in and Oswald's house was in serious danger of collapsing into the hole. However, the matter was promptly dealt with by Demolition Contractor Mouse who pulled Oswald's house down altogether, and so removed the danger.

Since Mouse got paid for all the jobs he did, he soon built up a vast fortune, and became Millionaire Mouse. When all the facts came to light he was accused of misusing public money and was brought to court. However, Magistrate Mouse said he did not see what all the fuss was about, and found him NOT GUILTY.